Meesh the BAD DEMON

The Secret of the Fang

ALSO BY MICHELLE LAM:

Meesh the Bad Demon: Volume 1

Meesh the BAD DEMON

The Secret of the Fang

MICHELLE LAM

WITH COLORS BY LAUREN "PERRY" WHEELER

ALFRED A. KNOPF  NEW YORK

THIS IS A BORZOI BOOK PUBLISHED BY ALFRED A. KNOPF

Visit us on the Web! rhcbooks.com

Educators and librarians, for a variety of teaching tools, visit us at RHTeachersLibrarians.com

Library of Congress Cataloging-in-Publication Data is available upon request.
ISBN 978-0-593-37291-3 (trade) — ISBN 978-0-593-37292-0 (lib. bdg.) —
ISBN 978-0-593-37293-7 (ebook) — ISBN 978-0-593-37290-6 (trade pbk.)

The text of this book is set in Caffe Lungo.
The illustrations were created using Photoshop.
Book design by Michelle Cunningham
With colors by Lauren "Perry" Wheeler

MANUFACTURED IN CHINA
10 9 8 7 6 5 4 3 2 1

First Edition

To my grandparents, Chow Yee Cheung,
Lai Cheung, Tsang Lam, and Yeung Ng Lam,
and my parents, Caren Cheung and Kenneth Lam,
for dealing with the REAL Meesh growing up.

PONDEROSA
WOW, CAN YOU BELIEVE WE'VE BEEN HERE FOR SIX MONTHS ALREADY?

IT'S NOT BAD FOR A TEMPORARY HOME, BUT . . .
MAYBE NEXT TIME WE CAN GET OUR REAL ONE BACK.
I PROMISE . . .
WE WILL.
POOF

CHAI, NO NEED TO OVEREXERT YOURSELF, OK? LET'S TAKE IT ONE STEP AT A TIME.
YES, DON'T WORRY, MY DEAR. WE WILL MAKE DO WITH WHAT WE HAVE FOR NOW.

BESIDES, HOW CAN YOU BEAT THIS VIEW?
WE WOLVES ARE STRONG. WE'LL GET THROUGH THIS AS A PACK.
YES!
AND NOW THAT WE HAVE THE SUPPORT OF MOUNT MAGMA AND PLUMERIA CITY, HOPEFULLY IT WON'T BE LONG.

HEY, REMEMBER— ONE STEP AT A TIME!

I KNOW, I KNOW!

A WOLF CAN DREAM, RIGHT?

SNIFF

WAIT, I SMELL SOMETHING OFF. . . .

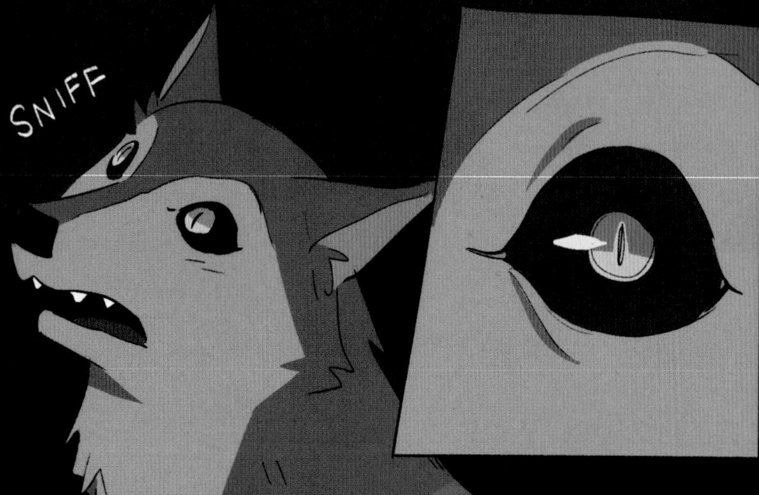

CHAI, RUN! NOW!
EVERYONE! EVACUATE THE AREA!
RUMBLE
GASP!
WHAM

FIRE?!
CRSSSHH

AH!
CHAI!

CHAI,
RUN!
WE'LL FIND YOU!

FWSSHHHH

MOUNT MAGMA
ONE, TWO, THREE—
HIT!

HAAA!

TSSS...

AH, WELL . . .

YOU GOT PART OF IT THIS TIME, BUT STILL MISSED A LOT.

WHAT?!

COME ON!
LET ME AT 'EM AGAIN!

NOW LET'S NOT BE HASTY.

HOW AM I SUPPOSED TO BE THE GUARDIAN WHEN I CAN'T DO ANYTHING?
MEESH, YOU CAN DO IT.
IT'S MORE ABOUT . . . REFINING!
YEAH, BUT THAT'S THE THING . . . ONE SMALL MISTAKE CAN RUIN EVERYTHING.
HEY, HEY. REMEMBER—
NO ONE JUST BECOMES THE GUARDIAN OVERNIGHT!

I MEAN, SURE, FOR YOU IT KIND OF WAS OVERNIGHT, TECHNICALLY.
MEESH, CAN I GET YOUR AUTO-GRAPH?!

BUT SKILLS TAKE TIME.
AND THAT'S OK!

THEN . . .
HOW LONG DID IT TAKE YOU TO GET GOOD AT IT?

SO . . .
DEPENDS ON WHAT YOU MEAN BY "IT."

HOW LONG DID IT TAKE FOR YOU TO STOP MAKING MISTAKES?
OH, I NEVER STOPPED MAKING MISTAKES.

WHAT DO YOU MEAN?
WELL . . .
POOF

REMEMBER THE JOB YOUR MOTHER HAD BACK THEN?

SHE WAS A LAVA SOURCER. EVERY DAY, SHE RISKED HER LIFE HIKING UP VOLCANOES TO HELP COLLECT THE PUREST LAVA.

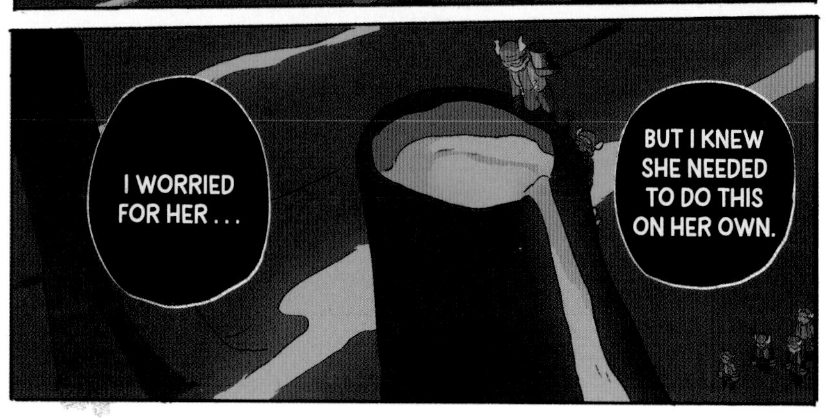

MEANWHILE, I HAD TO CONTINUE MY JOB AS GUARDIAN OF MOUNT MAGMA.

OVER TIME, I GUESS YOU COULD SAY BEING THE GUARDIAN BECAME . . .

DROP THE MONEY!

TEDIOUS.

BREAK IT UP!

BUT EVENTUALLY IT BECAME NO DIFFERENT THAN BEING THE MOUNT MAGMA POLICE.

IT'D BEEN YEARS SINCE MOUNT MAGMA HAD BEEN ATTACKED . . .
BY FAIRIES OR ANY OTHER MAJOR THREAT.

ANOTHER LONG DAY? YOU MISSED MEESH SAYING "MAMA"!
I WONDERED IF THE GUARDIAN WAS EVEN NECESSARY ANYMORE. . . .
WOULD YOU LIKE TO TRADE PLACES?

BE THE GUARDIAN? NO THANKS, I'M HAPPY HERE WITH MEESH! C'MON, JUST RETIRE ALREADY!
THEN MAYBE AT LEAST I CAN HEAR HER SAY "GRANDMAMA"!
WELL, THE OFFER IS THERE WHENEVER YOU WANT TO RETIRE FROM YOUR PARENTAL DUTIES!
HAHA!
AND THAT'S WHEN . . .

STAY OUT OF TROUBLE NEXT TIME!
WE'LL TAKE IT FROM HERE, GUARDIAN.
DID YOU HEAR THE NEWS? THERE WAS AN ACCIDENT . . .
WITH ONE OF THE LAVA SOURCERS. I THINK HER NAME WAS REN. . . .
SHE DROWNED AT THE VOLCANIC SITE.

I HEARD THE NEWS ABOUT YOUR MOTHER.
MY DAUGHTER.
AFTER THAT DAY . . .

BEING THE GUARDIAN NO LONGER MEANT ANYTHING TO ME.
ALL THAT TIME SPENT FIGHTING PETTY CRIMES . . .
MEESH, OPEN UP!
COULD HAVE BEEN SPENT WITH YOU AND YOUR MOTHER.
IT'S BUB-LAVA!

EVEN THOUGH I WAS THE GUARDIAN, I COULDN'T PROTECT YOUR MOTHER FROM WHAT HAPPENED.

YOU JUST STARTED DOING MAINTENANCE AT THE LAVA PLANT?

SO THAT'S WHY . . .

ANYWAY . . . WHAT I'M TRYING TO SAY IS, BEING THE GUARDIAN MAY SEEM EXCITING AND HIGH STAKES AND ALL . . .
BUT DON'T LET IT REPLACE WHO YOU ARE AND THOSE YOU LOVE. . . .
KNOCK KNOCK
WELL, LOOK WHO'S HERE!

HEY, MISS GUARDIAN! READY TO PRACTICE FLYING?
WHY DON'T YOU KIDS JUST GO HAVE SOME FUN?
OK, GRANDMA, I'LL SEE YOU LATER.
WANNA GO TO THE FOREST TODAY?
YEAH!

HEY, WAIT UP!
OH SHOOT, RIGHT.
FOR SOME REASON, I KEEP THINKING YOU CAN FLY, TOO!
YEAH, NOPE. THAT'S JUST THE GUARDIAN.
BUT HEY, FLYING IS LESS TURBULENT FOR BOTH OF YOU NOW!

AH, THERE IT IS!
WOOHOO, WE DID IT!
poof

LESS SHAKY, RIGHT, XAVIER? WE COULD TOTALLY MAKE IT FOR EVEN LONGER NEXT TIME!
UH, YEAH.
WELL, I GUESS YOU DON'T NEED ME ANYMORE. I'LL JUST HEAD HOME.
WHAT?!
BUT WE NEED TO PRACTICE ON THE WAY BACK, TOO!

WAAAH!

OH, I MET THESE TREES WHEN I RAN FROM MOUNT MAGMA THE FIRST TIME.
THEY'RE SAD WHEN YOU'RE SAD. BUT I WONDER WHY THEY'RE CRYING NOW?
UM, XAVIER? ARE YOU . . . ?
HUH?
IT'S REACHING FOR SOMETHING. . . .

CHAI?!
CHAI! WHAT HAPPENED TO YOU?!
CHAI!
XAVIER?

MEESH? NOUNA?
MY FAMILY! MY CAFÉ! I GOTTA–
WAIT!
WHAT HAPPENED?
Y-YOU'RE HURT!

Poof
IT . . .
IT'S HAPPENING AGAIN.
THAT PLACE ON TOP OF THE HILL . . . OUR TEMPORARY HOME. IT JUST GOT DESTROYED, TOO.
THERE WERE THESE BIG TRUCKS.
GIANT SHOVELS.

AND THEN I GOT SEPARATED FROM MY FAMILY.
WE'LL FIND YOU!
IT HAS TO BE HER. . . . THE SAME STRANGER XAVIER MET?
FIRST SHE TRIED TO DESTROY MOUNT MAGMA. AND NOW . . . MORE INNOCENT HOMES.
WE NEED TO FIND YOUR FAMILY, CHAI. LET'S MAKE SURE THEY'RE SAFE FIRST.

MAYBE NEAR THE CAFÉ? IT'S THE ONLY SPOT I CAN THINK OF.
OK, SO LET'S GO!
I CAN GO FIND THEM MYSELF. YOU GUYS SHOULD—
CHAI, YOU'VE HELPED US SO MUCH. NOW LET US HELP YOU. YOU'RE INJURED!
YEAH!
YOU HEARD THE GUARDIAN!
OK, YES, PLEASE.

BESIDES, I KNOW WHO CAN HELP US GET THERE QUICKER THAN FLYING THE WHOLE WAY WOULD. . . .

WOO!

NOUNA, WHEN I SAY SO, GET READY TO FLY!

WOO! HOO!

DID YOU ALWAYS KNOW THE TREES COULD DO THIS?
YEP! THAT'S HOW I FOUND PLUMERIA CITY THE FIRST TIME AROUND!
THERE'S PONDEROSA!

MY CAFÉ'S RIGHT THERE SOMEWHERE!
OK, NOUNA, ON THE COUNT OF THREE, YOU KNOW WHAT TO DO.
O-OK!
ONE . . . TWO . . .
THREE . . .
GO!

THANK YOU AGAIN, TREES!
WAVE
THAT'S IT RIGHT THERE!
MOM? MOM?

MOM!
CHAI . . .
OH NO, WHAT HAPPENED TO YOUR LEG?!

WE HAD A HARD TIME DODGING ALL OF THE FALLING TREES. . . .
SHE'LL PAY FOR THIS. . . .
I HAVE AN IDEA.

CAN YOU TELL US WHERE EXACTLY YOU LAST SAW THE DESTRUCTION HAPPENING?
THE OUTSKIRTS OF PONDEROSA.... IT MIGHT BE COMING THIS WAY NEXT....
XAVIER, CAN YOU TAKE CHAI AND HER FAMILY BACK TO MOUNT MAGMA FOR SHELTER?

WHAT?!
WHILE YOU
AND NOUNA
GO OUT AND
FIGHT?
YEAH, I WANT TO TAKE
DOWN WHOEVER DID THIS!

CHAI, YOU AND
YOUR FAMILY
RESTING AND
HEALING IS JUST
AS IMPORTANT
AS FINDING
OUT WHO IS
RESPONSIBLE.

AND, XAVIER, PLEASE,
WE NEED YOU TO TAKE THEM TO
MY GRANDMA. . . . SHE'LL KNOW
WHAT TO DO.

SIGH.

THANK YOU FOR OFFERING TO SHELTER US.

OH, YEAH.
IT'S THE LEAST WE COULD DO AFTER ALL YOU'VE DONE FOR US.
HEY, LOOK, I KNOW YOU'D RATHER BE OUT THERE WITH THEM, BUT . . .
YOU HELPING MY FAMILY MEANS MORE THAN YOU KNOW.
HEH.
WELL, THEN, LET'S GET GOING, SHALL WE?

I DIDN'T TRAIN TO HAVE ALL THIS STRENGTH FOR NOTHING.

MEANWHILE . . .
LOOK! THERE ARE MACHINERY TRACKS!

IT DOES LOOK LIKE WHAT CHAI WAS DESCRIBING. . . .
COUGH!

HERE!
SIR!
ARE YOU OK?
poof
WE CAN HELP YOU!
WHAT ARE YOU TWO YOUNGSTERS DOING HERE?

THEY'RE TEARING THIS PLACE APART!
NOT UNTIL WE GET TO THE BOTTOM OF THIS!
DO YOU KNOW WHO'S DOING THIS TO THE FOREST?
YOU HAVE TO LEAVE NOW!
THERE WERE THESE MASKED CONSTRUCTION WORKERS . . . WITH HORNS . . . AND WINGS! AT FIRST I THOUGHT IT COULDN'T BE. WE HAVEN'T SEEN FAIRY DEMONS IN YEARS!
FAIRY . . .
DEMONS?
AH, YOU KIDS ARE TOO YOUNG TO KNOW. THEY DISAPPEARED LONG BEFORE YOUR TIME.

WHY DON'T
YOU GO SEE FOR
YOURSELVES?

LOOK AT THOSE STONES . . .
THEY LOOK JUST LIKE . . .
MOUNT MAGMA AFTER IT WAS POISONED.

MOUNT MAGMA

KNOCK

MEESH?

OH . . .
SO YOU'RE TELLING ME . . .
MEESH AND NOUNA ARE OUT THERE RIGHT NOW?
THIS IS NOT GOOD. . . .
YES.
WHOEVER POISONED MOUNT MAGMA COULD ALSO BE TRYING TO DESTROY THE FORESTS . . . BUT WHY?

WE HAVE TO BRING THIS UP TO THE QUEEN OF PLUMERIA CITY.
THEY COULD ATTACK US AGAIN, OR PLUMERIA CITY MIGHT BE NEXT!
AND WHILE THE NIGHT IS ENDING FOR US, THE DAY IS STARTING FOR THEM.

I'LL GO ALERT PLUMERIA CITY.
WAIT, WE CAN COME WITH YOU, TOO!

NO, YOU TWO STAY HERE! CHAI, YOU LOOK AFTER YOUR FAMILY.
XAVIER, YOU SHOULD GO HOME TO YOUR MOTHER! GET SOME REST.

DOES EVERYONE SERIOUSLY THINK I'M JUST GONNA SIT AROUND IN MOUNT MAGMA AND DO NOTHING?!

XAVIER!

I'M TOTALLY WITH YOU, BUT . . . MAYBE WE SHOULD LISTEN?

HAVE YOU EVER HEARD OF "TOO MANY COOKS IN THE KITCHEN"?
YEAH, WELL, EVER SINCE MEESH BECAME THE GUARDIAN . . .
IT'S LIKE . . .
I'VE BECOME USELESS.
BEFORE THE WHOLE INCIDENT, I WAS AN A+ STUDENT, THE TOP OF OUR CLASS.
I HAD THE SKILLS TO DO SO MUCH.

AND NOW I'M JUST A PROP . . .
FOR WHEN MEESH AND NOUNA NEED TO PRACTICE.
WELL, YOU KNOW YOU'RE STILL EVERYTHING YOU WERE BEFORE, RIGHT?
BUT SOMETIMES WORKING AS A TEAM MEANS YOU HAVE TO DO THINGS FOR THE GREATER GOOD.

UGH, FINE! BUT IF I SEE ANY SIGN OF THAT LADY, I'M NOT JUST GONNA SIT BACK AND LET HER GET AWAY AGAIN.
WELL, THAT'S SOME CHARACTER DEVELOPMENT ON YOUR END!
HMPH.
BUT ANYWAY . . .
I WANTED TO TRY SOME OF THOSE DEMON SNACKS. . . .

PLUMERIA CITY

OH...
IT'S TIME.

CHOW?

MY QUEEN.

THE POISONING—IT'S BACK. BUT THIS TIME IT'S DIFFERENT.

ALREADY? WHAT'S GOING ON?
PONDEROSA'S FORESTS ARE BEING DESTROYED. AND THERE ARE TRACES OF THE POISON EVERYWHERE.

WE'LL HAVE TO EXPEDITE OUR PLANS TO MAKE SURE THIS DOESN'T HAPPEN AGAIN TO US OR TO PLUMERIA CITY.

I SEE. . . . YES, I AGREE, OF COURSE.

WHEN I SAW THE POISON IN MOUNT MAGMA . . .
IT REMINDED ME OF AN INCIDENT THAT HAPPENED HERE LONG AGO. . . .
SO, WE HAVE TO START NOW. GUARDS!
INCIDENT . . . ?

WE'LL NEED TO KEEP AN EYE OUT ON ALL ENTRYWAYS TO PLUMERIA CITY.
AND WE'LL NEED TO RECRUIT MORE GUARDS WITHIN THE CITY WALLS.
HUH.
WHERE IS LEON?

NOT SURE.
I HAVEN'T SEEN HIM IN A WHILE, EITHER. . . .
HMM . . .
WELL, FOR NOW, LET'S SPLIT UP AND GATHER MORE FAIRIES.
CHOW AND I WILL STRATEGIZE A PLAN OF ACTION.

THERE'S NO TIME TO WASTE!

PONDEROSA
UGH, WHAT SHOULD WE DO?
EVEN IF CHAI AND XAVIER HELP . . .
THERE'S NO WAY WE CAN RESOLVE THIS ALONE.

HOW ABOUT WE ASK YOUR GRANDMA AND MY MOM?

IT'D BE LIKE THE OLD GUARDIAN, NEW GUARDIAN, AND FAIRY QUEEN JOINING FORCES!

GRANDMA!

NO . . .
I CAN'T ASK MY GRANDMA TO DO THAT AGAIN. . . .

YOU'RE RIGHT.
I'M SORRY I BROUGHT IT UP.

NO, IT'S FINE.

BUT I THINK WE'RE ONTO SOMETHING.

LET'S GO BACK TO WHERE WE HAD THAT CAMPFIRE! THE CONSTRUCTION WORKERS ARE PROBABLY THERE!
UM . . . WHAT?
MEESH, I THINK YOU'RE BEING NAIVE.
WHAT, YOU THINK I'M JUST GONNA HAVE US GO LOOKING LIKE THIS?
HUH?
I'VE DONE IT ONCE, AND I CAN DO IT AGAIN. JUST FOLLOW ME!
WE'D MAKE THE PERFECT FAIRY DEMON!

UH . . . I STILL DON'T GET IT.
WELL, IT WILL MAKE SENSE LATER!
WOW, THEY REALLY DID A NUMBER ON THIS PLACE.

AW, MAN. ALL OUR PRECIOUS MEMORIES, JUST DESTROYED.

RUMBLE

YOU HEAR THAT?
YEAH.

IT'S PROBABLY ONE OF THE MACHINES. . . . LET'S FOLLOW IT.

UHH . . .

I'M NOT SURE ABOUT THIS. . . .

DO YOU SEE THAT?
WHOA . . .

WHAT ARE THEY BUILDING . . . ?
LOOKS LIKE SOME SORT OF LASER MACHINE?
BUT LOOK— THERE ARE FAIRIES WITH DEMON HORNS!
. . .
THOSE MUST BE THE FAIRY DEMONS.

COULD THEY ALL BE GUARDIANS, TOO? THEY HAVE HORNS AND WINGS LIKE YOU.
NO WAY.
THEIR WINGS ARE LIKE FAIRY WINGS.
WHICH IS WHY MY HORNS AND YOUR WINGS WOULD MAKE THE PERFECT DISGUISE!
WHAT?!
WHERE ARE YOU GOING?

SHHH.
THERE'S NO ONE IN THE TRUCK!
AHA!
SO THIS IS WHAT YOU MEANT BY A "DISGUISE"?!

YEP!
BUT WE CAUGHT YOU THE LAST TIME YOU DRESSED UP AS A FAIRY!
WELL, YOU LIVE AND YOU LEARN.
TRANSFER THESE TO THE BASE.
THEY'RE GONNA NEED MORE OF THESE TO BUILD THE LASER.

LASER . . . ?
FOLLOW HIM!
WHAT DO THEY MEAN, "LASER"?
HERE YOU GO!
THANKS!
GREAT, WE'LL NEED THIS FOR THE LEVER TO WORK.
YEP.
THAT'S WHAT IT'LL TAKE FOR THIS BABY TO BLOW UP PLUMERIA CITY.

N-NOUNA . . .
YOU HEARD
THAT, RIGHT?
Y-YEAH.
C'MON,
KEEP
ACTING
NORMAL!
PRETEND
TO PICK
SOMETHING
UP. DON'T
LOSE FOCUS!
WELL, IT'LL DEFINITELY LEVEL
ALL OF PONDEROSA FIRST.
GOOD THING WE ALREADY
WIPED OUT HALF OF IT
OURSELVES.
THIS THING
WILL JUST SPEED
UP THE PROCESS.
AND THEN WE'LL GET
MOUNT MAGMA
FOR GOOD.
YEAH. THEY
WERE LUCKY
THE FIRST
TIME.

UM . . . WE HAVE A BIG PROBLEM.
WH-WHAT SHOULD WE DO?
HEY, YOU!
UHHH.
YOU'VE GOT FREE HANDS, DON'T YOU?

HERE, GIMME THAT HAMMER. TAKE THESE TO THE BOTTOM OF THE BASE INSTEAD.
THANKS, BUDDY!
MEESH, I THINK WE'RE GONNA DIE CARRYING THIS.
bump

WHAT'S THE STATUS UPDATE FOR TODAY?

UHHH . . . WE FINISHED THE BASE OF THE . . . LASER?

STILL WAITING ON SOME MATERIALS TO BE DELIVERED!

OH, UH, THANK YOU.
LET ME HELP YOU THERE.
SEEMS A BIT HEAVY FOR SOMEONE YOUR SIZE.
WAIT. LEON?!
WHY DON'T WE ASSIGN YOU TO SOMETHING LIGHTER.

MEESH, DON'T DO IT.
DON'T FOLLOW HIM.
ISN'T THAT YOUR GUARD?
WELL, COME ALONG NOW.
NO!
HEY!

HEY!
GET BACK HERE!
I TOLD YOU THIS WAS A BAD IDEA!
I KNOW IT'S YOU—GUARDIAN AND PRINCESS NOUNA!
HUH?
WHAT'S GOING ON?
THERE'S BEEN A SECURITY BREACH!

HEY, AT LEAST WE GOT THE INFORMATION WE NEEDED!

AH!

NOUNA!
MEESH!
AH!

MEESH!
JUST HOLD ON!
GRAB THE PRINCESS!
I GOT HER!

HAAAAA!
CRK
HEY!

MEESH!

NOUNA! GO GET HELP!

WARN THE OTHERS!

AFTER HER!

KEEP FLYING!
KEEP FLYING!
KEEP FLYING!
FLY AROUND HER!
WE'LL BOX HER IN!

HEY!

THE BRANCHES ARE CLOSING IN!

HUFF.

HUFF.

BURN DOWN THE TREE IF YOU HAVE TO!

HURRY! BURN IT! GET HER!

RUMBLE

RAAA!

AH!

AHH!
WAAAH!
WHOA . . .

THANK YOU FOR THAT. . . .
AND ALSO, I WAS WONDERING . . .
DO YOU KNOW THE FASTEST WAY TO PLUMERIA CITY?
MEANWHILE . . .
UGH . . .

HELLO. IS ANYONE THERE?
DESTRUCTION PLAN
PLUMERIA CITY

WHA–

HAVE YOU SEEN HER?
WANTED
LOST
WELL, WELCOME . . .

MYSTERIOUS CREATURE IN BLACK SPOTTED IN PONDEROSA.

GUARDIAN OF MOUNT MAGMA.

PLUMERIA CITY

MOM! THE ONE WHO POISONED MOUNT MAGMA IS GOING TO BLOW UP PLUMERIA CITY WITH . . .
A LASER!
I SAW IT MYSELF!
WHAT? WHERE DID YOU GET THIS INFORMATION?
THERE WERE THESE DEMONS WITH FAIRY WINGS BUILDING IT.
AND THE WORST PART . . .
I SAW LEON WITH THEM.

TH-THERE'S NO WAY. . . .
IT CAN'T BE TRUE!
AND WHERE
IS MEESH?

UH,
MEESH . . .
SHE . . .
UH . . .

UHH,
MEESH IS
ACTUALLY
WAITING FOR ME
OUTSIDE! HAHA,
WHAT A BUSY
GUARDIAN SHE
IS. GOTTA GO!
WAIT,
NOUNA, IT'S
DANGEROUS!

I'LL BE BACK.
LET HER
GO. . . .
WAIT!

I KNOW IT'S TOUGH, BUT . . .
LET HER DO THIS ON HER OWN.

GULP.

MEANWHILE . . .
I'M ACTUALLY STARTING TO FEEL ENERGIZED.
DEMON CUISINE IS LITERALLY THE BEST.

THAT'S GOOD!

NOUNA?!

THUNK.

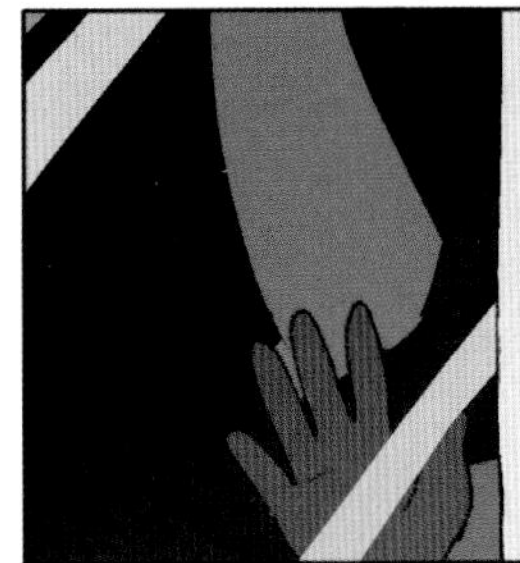

KNOCK
KNOCK

WHAT? SO YOUR OWN GUARD AND THESE FAIRY DEMONS KIDNAPPED MEESH?!

YEAH, SO, YOU SEE, I LIED TO MEESH'S GRANDMA AND SAID SHE'S OK. BUT . . .
SHE'S NOT. SO WE HAVE TO GET HER BACK.
I'LL NEED YOUR HELP.
YES, FINALLY! I CAN RIP THAT EVIL LADY TO SHREDS!
HEY!

CHAI, DO YOU THINK YOU'RE READY TO HELP?
I, UH . . .
I GOT THIS, OK?
MOM?!
I'LL GO WITH THEM.

YOU'RE NOT FULLY HEALED. REMEMBER— ONE STEP AT A TIME.
BESIDES, I WANT TO KNOW THE TRUTH BEHIND WHAT'S GOING ON.
THANK YOU, PRINCESS NOUNA, FOR LEADING THE WAY.
OH, UH, NO PROBLEM.
OK, WELL, HERE'S WHAT I'M THINKING FOR THE PLAN. . . .

WHO–
WHO ARE YOU?
ME?

I THINK THE BETTER QUESTION IS . . .
WHAT ARE YOU DOING STILL ALIVE?
T-TRYING TO STOP YOU . . .
FROM DESTROYING EVERYONE'S HOMES.
ME? DESTROY OTHERS' HOMES?

YOU DON'T KNOW THE SLIGHTEST THING ABOUT HAVING YOUR HOME TAKEN AWAY.
MA'AM, A WORKER HAS BEEN INJURED!
SHE WAS CAUGHT IN THE CROSSFIRE WITH THE GUARDIAN AND THE PRINCESS.
ONE OF THOSE TREES ATTACKED HER!
OH MY.
WE'LL MAKE SURE TO BURN DOWN EACH AND EVERY TREE.

BUT FIRST, ARE YOU ALL RIGHT?
DON'T WORRY, MS. EVA. A FEW BRUISES WON'T KEEP ME DOWN.
NO NEED TO PLAY TOUGH. HERE, LET ME HEAL YOU.
IT WILL REDUCE THE PAIN.
TH-THANK YOU.
TAKE HER TO THE RECOVERY ROOM.
WILL DO.
ONE HEALING ELIXIR EVERY MORNING FOR THE NEXT THREE DAYS.
FEEL BETTER SOON.
THANK YOU AGAIN!
WHAT . . . ?

FAIRY DEMONS ARE RESILIENT CREATURES.
IT WOULD TAKE A LOT TO TAKE US DOWN.
N-NO.
I THOUGHT YOU WERE EVIL. . . .
EVIL? HUH.
OF COURSE, YOU'RE TOO YOUNG TO UNDERSTAND.

AND YET YOU'RE STILL NO DIFFERENT FROM THE DEMONS AND FAIRIES OF MOUNT MAGMA AND PLUMERIA CITY.
DEMONS?!
FAIRIES?!
YOU'RE THE ONES WHO POISONED US!
EVEN PLUMERIA CITY IS ON OUR SIDE!
WHAT DO YOU MEAN?
WE KNOW WHAT YOU TRIED TO DO. YOU WANTED US DEMONS TO THINK IT WAS THE FAIRIES' FAULT!
OUR WORLDS MAY HAVE HAD A ROUGH HISTORY UNTIL NOW TO HIDE WHAT WAS REALLY YOUR DOING ALL ALONG!

YOU THINK I'M THE PROBLEM WHEN THAT'S FAR FROM . . .
THE TRUTH.
MANY YEARS AGO . . .
PLUMERIA CITY WAS AT ITS PEAK LONG BEFORE YOU WERE BORN.
OUR PRODUCE WAS FRESHER THAN EVER.
OUR CITY GREW FASTER THAN IT EVER HAD.
AND BUSINESSES WERE FLOURISHING.

WINGED CREATURES FROM EVERYWHERE ONCE CALLED PLUMERIA CITY HOME.
THERE WERE EVEN . . .
FAIRY DEMONS.

WE ALL HAPPILY COEXISTED.
CONGRATS TO THIS YEAR'S WINNING SCULPTOR!
OUR UNIQUE POWERS WERE CELEBRATED.
LIFT!
WINNER
LOOK, I MADE A FISH!
SO . . .
YOU'RE ALSO . . . A FAIRY DEMON?

WHOOSH
THAT'S RIGHT.
WHA–
AH!
AND THAT'S NOT THE END OF THE STORY.

WHAT'S THIS?
OUR CROPS ARE ALL DEAD! WE CAN NEVER SELL THESE. . . .
NOTHING GOOD LASTS FOREVER. PLUMERIA CITY LEARNED THAT THE HARD WAY.
SORRY, NO PRODUCE TODAY.
I KNOW YOU HATE DEMON GRITS, BUT LET'S JUST MAKE THE BEST OF IT.
UGH, THIS LITERALLY LOOKS LIKE PUKE.
ATTENTION: BREAKING NEWS!

PLUMERIA CITY IS FACING THE LARGEST FOOD SHORTAGE IN ITS HISTORY.
NEWS
BREAKING NEWS
IN ONLY A MATTER OF MONTHS, THE CITY WILL OFFICIALLY BE IN A . . .
STAGE 4 FAMINE EMERGENCY.
IT'S BELIEVED THAT THE SPORES OF FAIRY DEMONS ARE POISONING THE PLANTS.
WE WON'T KNOW FOR SURE UNTIL ALL POSSIBLE CAUSES ARE INVESTIGATED.
SO FOR NOW, THE QUEEN IS ASKING ALL FAIRY DEMONS . . .

TO PLEASE VACATE PLUMERIA CITY.
BUT WE DON'T HAVE ANY SPORES!
YOU CAN'T DO THIS TO US. THIS IS OUR HOME, TOO!
LUCKILY, MY FATHER HAD DEMON FRIENDS LIVING IN MOUNT MAGMA.
WELCOME TO OUR HUMBLE ABODE!

HERE, I CAN TAKE THAT.
WE KNEW THOSE FAIRIES WERE UP TO NO GOOD! DEMONS OF ANY KIND ALWAYS GET THE BRUNT END OF THE STICK WITH THEM.
WELL, THEY DID SAY THAT IT WOULD ONLY BE TEMPORARY.
WE'LL BE BACK THERE IN NO TIME ONCE THINGS ARE RESOLVED.
WEEKS PASSED, AND THERE WAS NO HOPE OF RETURNING TO PLUMERIA CITY.

WATCH IT, FAIRY!
IGNORE THESE ROAD RAGERS, EVE.
IN MANY WAYS, MOUNT MAGMA WAS WORSE THAN PLUMERIA CITY FOR FAIRY DEMONS.
MEAT
EGGS
FROZEN
SPORES.
WATCH OUT FOR THEIR SPORES.
AREN'T WINGS FOR FAIRIES?
SHE'S A SPORE!
I HATE MY SCHOOL, I HATE MOUNT MAGMA!
THIS IS UNACCEPTABLE. I'M GOING TO ASK YOUR SCHOOL FOR THEIR PARENTS' INFORMATION.

I'LL GO TALK TO THEM.
THEY SHOULD KNOW THAT WE ARE DEMONS, TOO!
NO, DAD!
THEY'RE ONLY GONNA PICK ON ME MORE–
AH!
TSHHH

EVE!

DO THAT AGAIN AND YOU'RE GROUNDED!

BUT . . .

I'LL BE BACK SOON, SO STAY PUT!

HUH, THESE ARE THE SAME FRUITS WE ATE IN PLUMERIA CITY. . . .

WE'VE BEEN HERE FOR WEEKS, AND THEY'RE STILL PERFECTLY RIPE?!
I THOUGHT OUR SPORES . . .
WAS IT ALL A LIE?
I NEED TO GO SHOW DAD!
EVA, LET'S WAIT FOR YOUR DAD TO GET BACK FIRST.

COME ON, IT'S TIME TO HEAD INSIDE.
BUT . . .

HE'LL BE BACK BEFORE YOU KNOW IT.

I WAITED ALL NIGHT, BUT MY FATHER NEVER CAME BACK.

YOU CAN'T BE SERIOUS!
WHAT DO YOU MEAN, HE WAS . . .
KILLED?

SHHH, BE QUIET! EVA WILL HEAR!
THE DEMON PARENT ATTACKED HIM . . .
OUT OF FEAR OF HIS SPORES?!
YOU REALIZE HIS DAUGHTER WAS THE ONE BEING BULLIED BY THEIR KID . . . ?
HOW AM I SUPPOSED TO TELL HER THAT HER FATHER IS GONE?

I KNEW IF I WAS GOING TO ESCAPE MOUNT MAGMA . . .
SORRY, UNCLE.
SORRY, AUNTIE.

I COULD NO LONGER LET OTHERS KNOW I WAS A FAIRY DEMON.
OR ELSE I COULD BE NEXT.
EVA, SWEETIE? ARE YOU IN . . .
THERE . . . ?

N-NO . . .
SHE COULDN'T HAVE . . .
FEAR GREW AMONG THE FAIRY DEMONS LIVING IN MOUNT MAGMA.
DID THEY REALLY JUST RIP OFF HIS HORNS AND HIS WINGS?
WE NEED TO GET OUT OF HERE AS SOON AS POSSIBLE.
IT EVENTUALLY DROVE THEM OUT. THEY HEADED TO PONDEROSA FOR A LAST CHANCE AT A NEW LIFE.

BUT I HAD OTHER PLANS IN MIND. . . .
WHO ARE YOU?
I'M EVALINA SCULPTOR. I USED TO LIVE HERE!
AND I'M HERE TO SHOW YOU THE TRUTH! FAIRY-DEMON SPORES DIDN'T POISON THE CROPS IN PLUMERIA CITY!

IT HAD TO BE . . .
SOMETHING ELSE THAT DESTROYED THEM HERE!
GASP!
SO PLEASE LET US ALL COME HOME! FAIRY DEMONS AREN'T WELCOME IN MOUNT MAGMA.
MY FATHER . . . HE WAS KILLED DOWN THERE.
WH- WHAT?!
GUARDS!
COME HERE IMMEDIATELY!
SORRY, MISS, YOU'LL HAVE TO LEAVE NOW.
BUT WAIT! I'M TELLING THE TRUTH!

YOU CAN'T JUST KICK US OUT OF OUR HOMES LIKE THIS!
HUH?
NOUNA STUDIOS
N-NOUNA STUDIOS?!
NOUNA STUDIOS
A TV STUDIO?!
THAT . . .

YOU BUILT A TV STUDIO . . .
ON TOP OF OUR HOUSE?!
GO HOME!
AND DON'T COME BACK!
AHH!
AND THAT'S WHEN I ASKED MYSELF, "HOME?"

WHAT HOME?
I WAS A FOOL TO THINK THAT PLUMERIA CITY WAS EVER MY HOME.
DRIP
DRIP
AND SO THEN . . .

GREEN STRIPES?
HA!
HNG!
I BUILT MY OWN HOME.

AND IT DIDN'T TAKE TOO LONG UNTIL . . .
DID YOU BUILD THIS ALL BY YOURSELF?
I MEAN, WE HAVE NO OTHER CHOICE, RIGHT?
HERE, LET ME SHOW YOU.

WHOA!
H-HOW DID YOU MAKE THOSE GREEN STRIPES?
I'M NOT REALLY SURE.
REGARDLESS, YOU'RE QUITE TALENTED.
WOW! YOU KNOW HOW TO BUILD A SHELTER!

SOON MORE FAIRY DEMONS FLEEING MOUNT MAGMA AND PONDEROSA EMERGED, SEEKING SHELTER.

WHY NOT USE OUR GIFT OF "SPORES" TO CREATE A NEW PLACE? ONE THAT COULD BE HOME.

THE CREATURES IN PONDEROSA HAVE BEEN MORE UNFORGIVING LATELY.
BE CAREFUL OUT THERE.
I WENT TO SEARCH FOR THE REMAINING FAIRY DEMONS.
I WANTED TO MAKE SURE THAT WHAT HAPPENED TO MY FATHER NEVER HAPPENED TO ANOTHER FAIRY DEMON EVER AGAIN.

PONDEROSA WAS SUPPOSED TO BE A CITY FOR ALL CREATURES . . .
OR AT LEAST THAT'S WHAT WE WERE TOLD.
PLEASE LET ME WORK HERE! I NEED TO SUPPORT MY SON!
SORRY, SIR, BUT WE HEARD ABOUT WHAT HAPPENED TO PLUMERIA CITY. WE CAN'T RISK IT, EITHER.
BUT WHAT YOU HEARD ISN'T TRUE. JUST GIVE US A CHANCE.

SLAM
CLOSED

YOU DON'T NEED THEM.

COME WITH ME. I'LL TAKE YOU TO A PLACE WHERE IT'S SAFE FOR US.

Y-YOU'RE . . . THE MASKED HERO. . . .
YOU'RE ACTUALLY . . . REAL?

THANK YOU SO MUCH. WE HAD ALMOST GIVEN UP HOPE OF EVER FINDING YOU OR YOUR LOCATION.

WHAT DO YOU MEAN?
IT'S A SECRET FOR A REASON.

W-WHOA! THE GROUND— IT'S—
SINKING?!
HUH?

HEY! WELCOME! YOU MUST BE ABSOLUTELY EXHAUSTED. HERE, HAVE A DRINK.
EAT UP AND RELAX. YOU'RE FINALLY HOME.
WE'RE SAFE HERE? REALLY?
TH- THANK YOU!
WE TOOK OUR HOME UNDERGROUND TO AVOID EVER LOSING IT AGAIN.

BESIDES . . .

THOSE FAIRY DEMONS STOPPED KNOCKING ON MY DOOR.

DID THEY SERIOUSLY THINK I COULD AFFORD SO MANY LIABILITIES?

YEAH, I ACTUALLY HAVEN'T SEEN ANY OF THEM IN A WHILE.

IT'S REALLY A SHAME THAT EVERYONE FOUND US USELESS—

WH-WHERE ARE YOU TAKING ME?!

HAVE THE POWER TO CREATE.

YOU AND THE PRINCESS MAY HAVE SAVED MOUNT MAGMA . . .

BUT DON'T EVER MISTAKE YOURSELVES FOR HEROES.

N-NO! STOP!

HNG . . .

AND YOU THINK POISONING MOUNT MAGMA MAKES YOU THE HERO?!
AH . . .
SO THAT'S WHERE THE POWER OF THE GUARDIAN COMES FROM.

JUST BECAUSE YOU'VE BEEN HURT . . .
A SMALL, FRAGILE FANG.
DOESN'T MEAN YOU CAN GO HURT OTHERS!
YOU ALREADY FORGOT . . .

THAT I'M ALSO HALF DEMON!
WHAT'S GOING ON . . . ?
I CAN'T . . . HOLD ON. . . .
AH!

NOT SO FAST!

WHAT DO YOU EVEN WANT FROM ME?!
ARGH!!
AHHH!

I'M SORRY ABOUT WHAT HAPPENED IN MOUNT MAGMA, BUT . . .
THE GUARDIAN DIDN'T HAVE ANYTHING TO DO WITH IT!
AND THAT'S EXACTLY WHAT WENT WRONG!
YOU DON'T UNDERSTAND!
HA!
zzZZZZZ

GAH!
THNK
MY MOM. SHE WAS THE REASON MY GRANDMA GAVE UP BEING THE GUARDIAN.
HUH?
IF ONLY I KNEW ABOUT YOUR FANG IN THE FIRST PLACE . . .
MAYBE I WOULDN'T HAVE HAD TO POISON MOUNT MAGMA . . .

AND THEN YOUR GRANDMA COULD HAVE HAPPILY ENJOYED HER RETIREMENT.
BUT SHE CHOSE TO LET EVERYONE SUFFER.

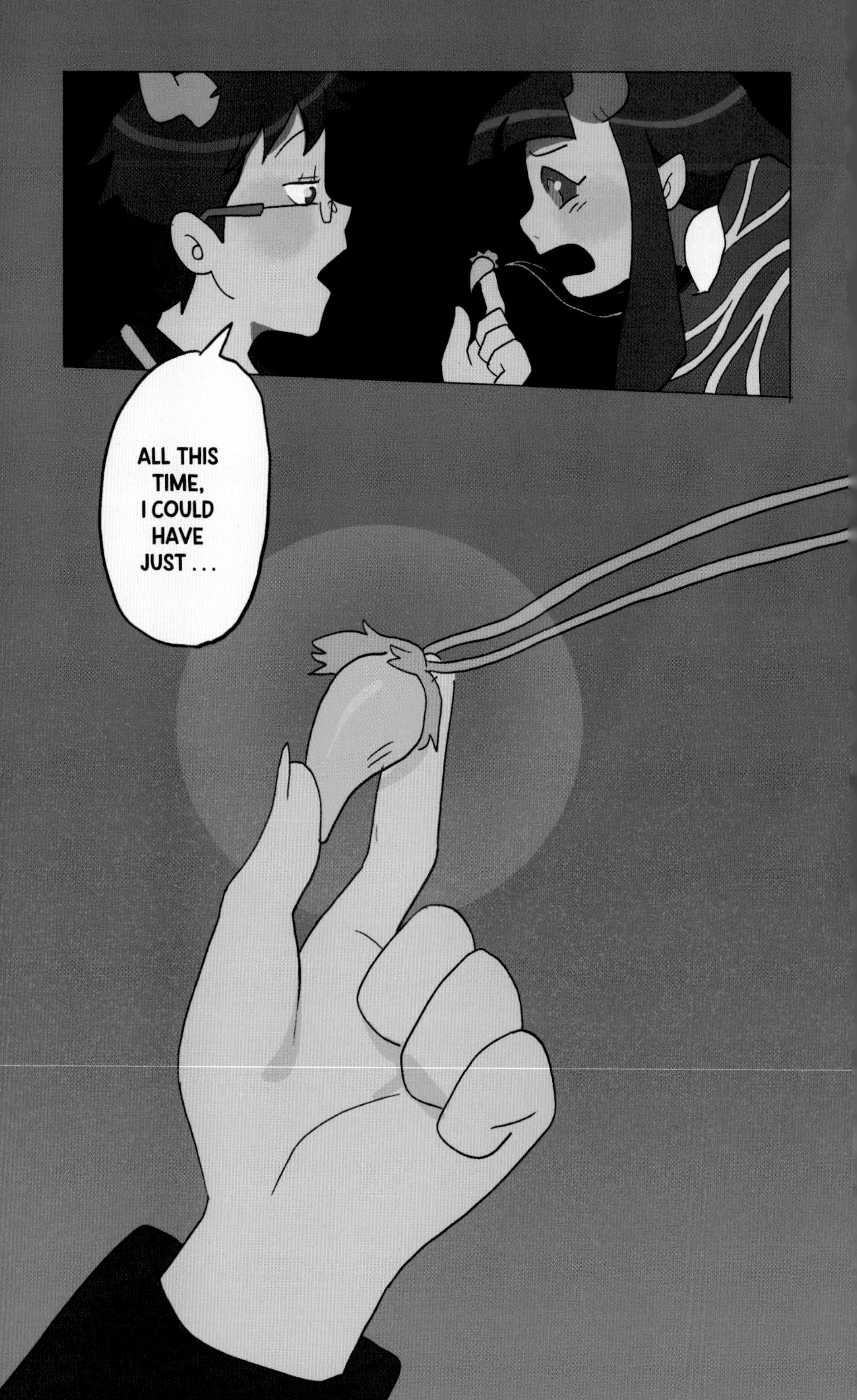
ALL THIS TIME, I COULD HAVE JUST . . .

DESTROYED THIS INSTEAD.

CR

SH

NOOO!!!

FWSHHHH
NO, NO!
MY WINGS!
MY HORNS!
I'M . . .
NORMAL.

YOU'RE BETTER OFF THAT WAY, DON'T YOU THINK?

NOW THIS, EVERYONE, IS THE GUARDIAN OF MOUNT MAGMA!
OR SHALL I SAY, *WAS.*
FROM THIS DAY ONWARD, WE WILL NO LONGER BE INVISIBLE TO FAIRIES AND TO DEMONS.

IS THIS REALLY A GOOD IDEA?!
I DON'T KNOW. . . . SHE'S JUST A KID.
ISN'T THIS A BIT MUCH?
KINDA CRUEL?
MY GRANDMA MAY NOT HAVE KNOWN WHAT WAS HAPPENING TO YOU . . . BUT IF I HAD, I PROMISE I WOULD NEVER HAVE LET THIS HAPPEN TO THE FAIRY DEMONS.

THNK

PLUMERIA CITY
SO . . . THAT'S WHY THE FAIRY DEMONS MIGRATED TO MOUNT MAGMA. . . .
I STAYED OUT OF ALL WORLD AFFAIRS ONCE I QUIT MY GUARDIAN DUTIES.
I DON'T BLAME YOU FOR THAT, BUT I STILL FEEL AWFUL.

AFTER NOUNA WAS BORN, I COULDN'T RISK A FAMINE IN PLUMERIA CITY.
ESPECIALLY WITH HER BROKEN WING ALREADY MAKING HER SO VULNERABLE.
BUT IT TURNED OUT THAT THE CROP FAILURE WAS DUE TO OUR OWN OVER-FARMING DURING THE GOLDEN ERA.

NOUNA
STUDIOS
WE WERE TOO ASHAMED TO ADMIT WE WERE WRONG.
SO WE CONSTRUCTED NEW BUILDINGS AND BROUGHT IN IMPORTS TO HIDE OUR MISTAKES.
BUT AFTER SEEING HOW MEESH AND NOUNA SAVED MOUNT MAGMA, I KNEW I COULDN'T KEEP IGNORING THE REMAINING PUZZLE PIECE.
BUT IT FEELS TOO LATE TO MAKE AMENDS NOW.
IT WASN'T TOO LATE FOR YOU TO HELP MOUNT MAGMA.

IT WON'T BE TOO LATE TO HELP THE FAIRY DEMONS.
OUR WORLDS MAY HAVE A FRAUGHT HISTORY, BUT THIS IS WHERE WE COME TOGETHER TO MAKE THINGS RIGHT.
NOT JUST BETWEEN PLUMERIA CITY AND MOUNT MAGMA . . .
BUT WITH THE FAIRY DEMONS, WITH PONDEROSA, AND WITH EVERYONE ELSE AS WELL.
AND HERE I THOUGHT YOU HAD TRULY QUIT BEING THE GUARDIAN.
YOU JUST GAVE ME AN IDEA.

GUARDS, THERE'S BEEN A CHANGE OF PLANS.
WE WILL HEAD OUT TO FIND THOSE THREATENING PLUMERIA CITY OURSELVES.
LEAVE PLUMERIA CITY? YOUR HIGHNESS, IS THAT SAFE?!

WE HAVE TO MAKE THINGS RIGHT WITH THE FAIRY DEMONS.
THEY'RE THE ONES WHO–
HELENA.
IT'S TIME WE STOP VIEWING OUR WORLD AS THE ONLY WORLD.
CAN I TRUST YOU, MY LONGEST-SERVING GUARD, TO DEFEND PLUMERIA CITY IF IT COMES TO THAT?
YES, YOUR HIGHNESS.

VERY WELL. WE'LL BE BACK AS SOON AS WE CAN!
EXHALE
OK, GUARDS!
YOU HEARD THE QUEEN!
AND YOU REMEMBER WHAT FAIRY DEMONS ARE CAPABLE OF!

drip
UGH . . .
WHA . . . ?
WHERE AM I?!

NOT EVEN A SCRATCH . . .
OF COURSE, I CAN'T DO ANYTHING WITHOUT MY FANG NOW. . . .
YOU STUPID DEMON!
BANG!

HOW COULD I HAVE LET THIS HAPPEN . . . ?
YOU'LL BREAK YOUR HANDS IF YOU KEEP DOING THAT.
LEON . . .
HOW COULD YOU DO THIS?! BETRAY NOUNA AND ALL OF PLUMERIA CITY?!

BUT I DON'T UNDERSTAND THE POINT OF KEEPING ME HOSTAGE . . .

WHEN I CAN'T EVEN DO ANYTHING ANYMORE!

TRUST ME, IT'S NOT LIKE I WANTED THINGS TO END UP THE WAY THEY ARE WITH YOU AND YOUR FRIENDS.
MY . . .
FRIENDS?
MEANWHILE . . .
THIS IS WHERE IT HAPPENED.
THOSE STRIPED ROCKS!
BUT LOOK FURTHER!

IS THAT . . . A LASER MACHINE?
THE ONE THAT'S GOING TO BLOW UP PLUMERIA CITY? YEP.
AND THAT ALSO MEANS THAT MEESH CAN'T BE TOO FAR AWAY.
HUH?

MEESH'S FANG?

IT CAN'T BE . . .

MEESH'S FANG . . .

I'M SURE WE CAN FIX IT!
RIGHT?
AH!
CRK
THAT WAS CLOSE.

LOOK OUT BEHIND YOU!
AH!!!
OOF!
THNK

AND THAT'S WHEN WE FELL . . .

INTO MY TRAP.

I AM A FAIRY DEMON.

ALL THIS TIME . . . YOU LIED TO US?!

NO WAY.

CAN YOU REALLY BLAME HIM FOR LYING, THOUGH?
WELL, THEY'RE OUT OF YOUR WAY NOW. ENTER PHASE THREE?
YES.
AFTER WE FINISH THEM FOR GOOD.

WAIT, WHAT?! EVA, I THOUGHT WE CHANGED THE PLAN.
YOU SAID WE'D ONLY HOLD THEM UNTIL IT'S OVER.
WELL, I GUESS THAT MAKES BOTH OF US LIARS.
WHAT?!
BUT THEY'RE JUST KIDS!
PEW

WHAT . . . ?
KA
POOM

TSSS...
WHAT ARE YOU DOING?!
WHAT ARE YOU DOING?!
YOU CAN'T KEEP CHANGING THE PLAN LIKE THIS!
I'VE HAD ENOUGH!

THIS CELL WAS SUPPOSED TO KEEP THEM OUT OF THE DESTRUCTION PLAN!

YOU SAID YOU'D LEAVE THE PRINCESS AND HER FRIENDS OUT OF THIS IF WE CAUGHT THEM ALL.

WELL, THEN . . .

IF YOU DON'T BELIEVE IN MY PLAN—OUR PLAN—THEN WHY DON'T YOU GO JOIN THEM INSTEAD?

THERE WAS NEVER AN "OUR" PLAN.

WILL MY WINGS LOOK LIKE YOURS SOMEDAY?
NO. ONLY A PRINCESS HAS WINGS AS UNIQUE AS YOURS.
REALLY?!
HAPPY BIRTHDAY, LITTLE LEON!
WHEE!

RUN!
GO! GET OUT OF HERE!
WHAT?!
HURRY! GO NOW IF YOU WANT TO SAVE YOURSELVES!

COME ON!
LET'S GO!

LEON!

AH!

LEON . . .
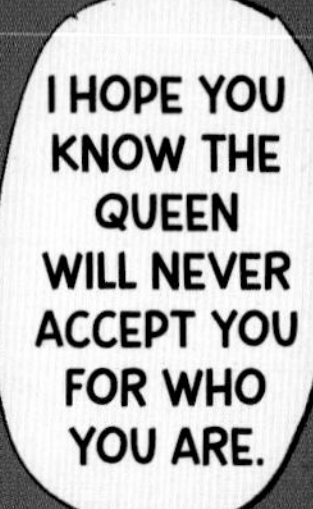
I HOPE YOU KNOW THE QUEEN WILL NEVER ACCEPT YOU FOR WHO YOU ARE.

I KNOW.

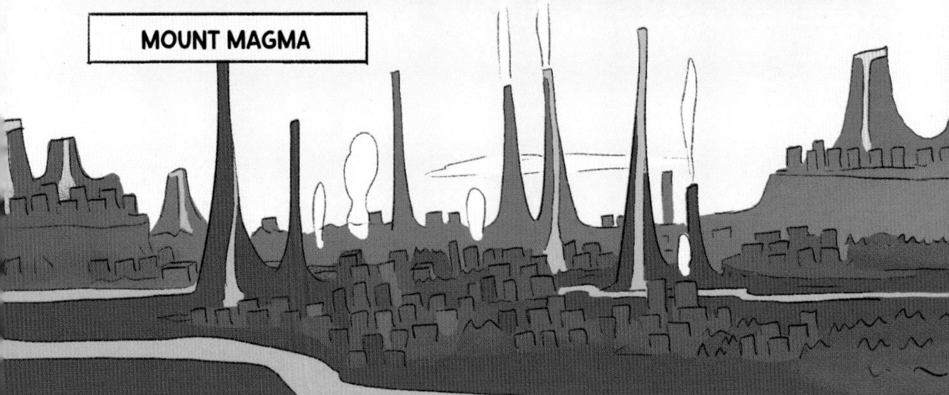
MOUNT MAGMA

HOW'S YOUR ARM DOING?
I THINK IT'S HEALED, DON'T YOU?

THIS SHOULD NEVER HAVE HAPPENED. WE SHOULD HAVE KNOWN TO FIND A MORE SECURE LOCATION BEFORE ATTEMPTING TO SETTLE DOWN.

IT WOULD HAVE BEEN THE BEST WAY TO KEEP YOU SAFE.
SAFE?! ARE YOU KIDDING ME?
I WOULDN'T HAVE MET MEESH OR NOUNA IF ALL WE'D WORRIED ABOUT WAS STAYING HIDDEN.
AND BESIDES, I GET TO MEET SO MANY NEW CREATURES FROM EVERYWHERE AT THE CAFÉ. IT'S HELPED ME FIND MYSELF.

WE MAY HAVE MOVED
AROUND A LOT, BUT IT TAUGHT ME
SO MUCH ABOUT THE WORLD.
IT MADE ME WONDER . . .
MAYBE ALL THIS TIME, "HOME"
WAS NEVER A PLACE.

I GOT A LOT OF NEW IDEAS FOR MY CAFÉ, TOO, THANKS TO THE SNACKS IN MEESH'S GRANDMA'S KITCHEN!
CHAI!
THAT'S OUR CHAI!
THEY'RE BACK ALREADY?!
COME ON, OPEN UP!
WHAT HAPPENED TO ALL OF YOU?

ARE YOU ALL . . . OK . . . ?
HUFF.
HUFF.
WHO DID THIS TO YOU?!
IT'S THE FAIRY DEMONS.
THEY BUILT A WHOLE CITY IN THE GROUND BENEATH OUR HOME.

SO ALL OF PLUMERIA CITY AND PONDEROSA . . . WILL BE DESTROYED?!
YEAH. EVA, THEIR LEADER, IS ACTING OUT OF REVENGE FOR WHAT HAPPENED TO THE FAIRY DEMONS.
ONCE THE LASER COMES TO THE SURFACE . . .
IT WILL WIPE OUT EVERYTHING STANDING IN ITS WAY.

YIKES . . .

BUT YOU AND NOUNA CAN DO WHAT YOU DID LAST TIME TO SAVE US, RIGHT?

UH, ABOUT THAT . . .

PLEASE TELL ME YOU CAN. . . .

SO EVEN IF NOUNA TRIED TO USE HER OLD RUBY LIKE LAST TIME . . .
I WOULDN'T HAVE MY FANG TO HELP.
TAKING DOWN EVA WILL BE WAY MORE OF A CHALLENGE THAN RESTORING MOUNT MAGMA WAS. MAYBE EVEN IMPOSSIBLE NOW.
AND BESIDES, I DON'T THINK I WAS MEANT TO BE THE GUARDIAN.
A TRUE GUARDIAN WOULD'VE NEVER LET THAT FANG FALL INTO THE WRONG HANDS.

BUT HEY, NOUNA CAN DO THINGS WITHOUT HER RUBY NOW, CHAI IS AN EXTRAORDINARY WEREWOLF, AND XAVIER IS THE #1 DEMON STUDENT IN CLASS.
YOU'LL ALL PROBABLY BE ABLE TO DO MORE THAN I EVER COULD.
WHO SAID YOU WERE GOING TO DO THIS ALL ALONE, HUH?!

YOU REALLY THINK YOU'RE GONNA LEAVE THE DIRTY WORK TO US?!
LET'S NOT FORGET YOUR FANG WASN'T WORKING THE LAST TIME, EITHER!
CAN'T YOU SEE? ALL THIS TIME, YOUR POWER JUST CAME FROM YOU!

YEAH, BUT . . .
IT ONLY CAME FROM ME BECAUSE I WAS PROUD TO BE A DEMON. . . .
BUT HOW CAN I BE PROUD NOW THAT I KNOW DEMONS HAVE HURT FAIRY DEMONS SO MUCH?

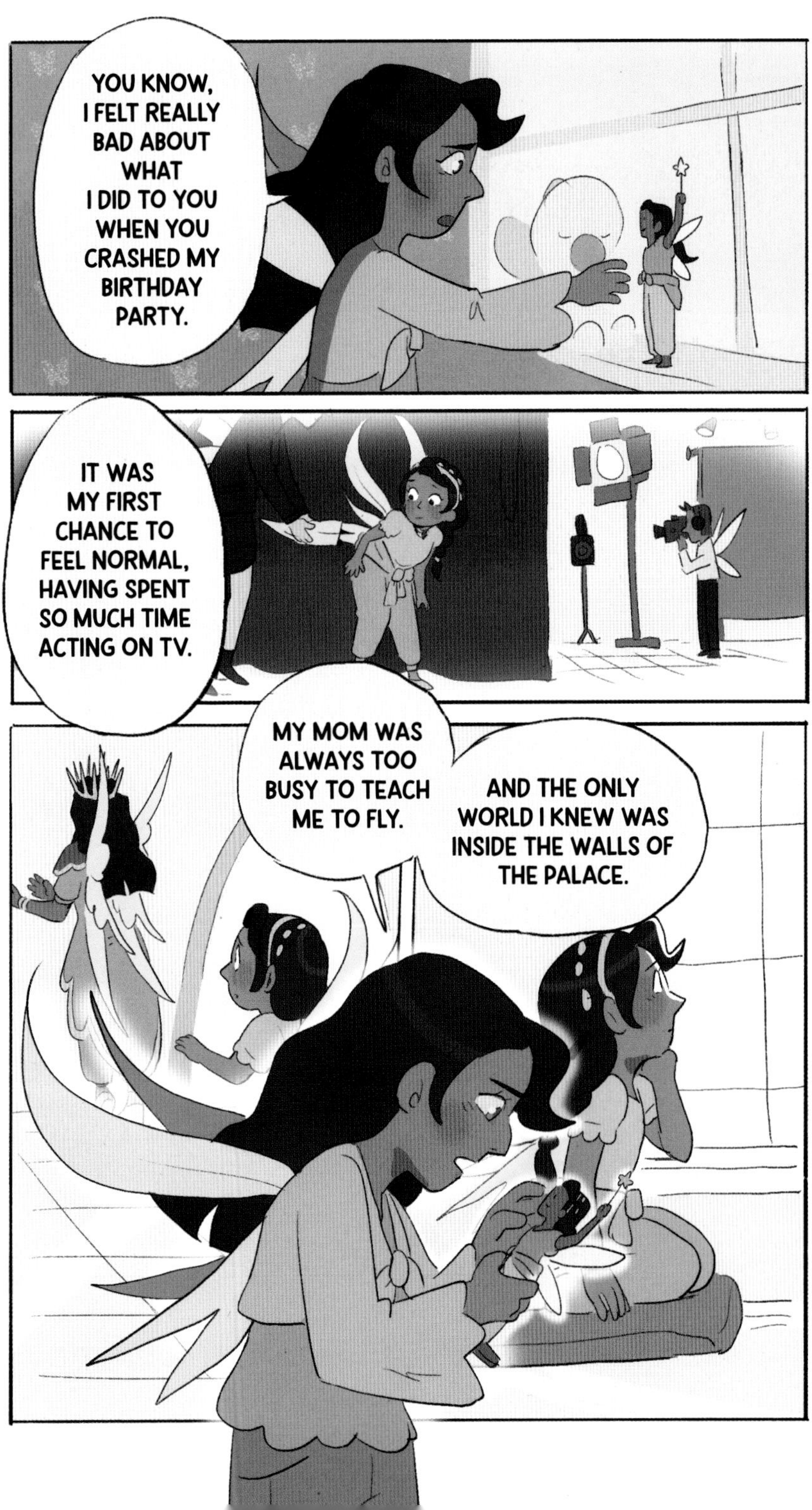

IT WAS MY FIRST CHANCE TO FEEL NORMAL, HAVING SPENT SO MUCH TIME ACTING ON TV.

MY MOM WAS ALWAYS TOO BUSY TO TEACH ME TO FLY.

AND THE ONLY WORLD I KNEW WAS INSIDE THE WALLS OF THE PALACE.

BUT AFTER YOU FOUND OUT THE TRUTH ABOUT PLUMERIA CITY, AND THE TRUTH ABOUT ME . . .
YOU STILL BELIEVED I COULD DO SOMETHING GOOD. 
EVEN WHEN YOU FIGURED OUT THAT THE PRINCESS NOUNA ON TV ISN'T LIKE THE REAL ME.

YOU DIDN'T GIVE UP ON ME, SO DON'T GIVE UP ON YOURSELF.

THANKS, NOUNA.

MEESH, I ALSO—

LEON?! HOW DID YOU—
WAIT, WAIT! I'M NOT HERE TO HURT YOU, OK?

AND HOW ARE WE SUPPOSED TO BELIEVE THAT?!
LOOK, I KNOW I HID THE FACT THAT I'M A FAIRY DEMON. . . .
IT'S NOT BECAUSE YOU'RE A FAIRY DEMON!
IT'S BECAUSE YOU LIED TO AND BETRAYED US!
YOU'RE RIGHT. I'M SORRY I LIED. SO PLEASE LET ME TELL YOU THE TRUTH.
THE TRUTH?

I, AS WELL AS A FEW OTHER FAIRY DEMONS, MANAGED TO LAY LOW IN PLUMERIA CITY AFTER THE EXILE. . . .
SOME OF US COULD, IF OUR HORNS WERE SMALL ENOUGH TO HIDE.
MY FAMILY WAS EXILED, BUT THEY URGED ME TO STAY BEHIND. TO FIGHT FOR A BETTER LIFE.
AND THAT'S WHEN I LANDED MY JOB AS A FAIRY GUARD. I WAS ABLE TO GET ALL OF THE INTEL ON PLUMERIA CITY'S PLANS . . .
BUT I NEVER HEARD ANYTHING ABOUT WELCOMING THE FAIRY DEMONS BACK.

ONCE THE "SPORES" MYTH WAS DEBUNKED, I WENT OUT TO SEARCH FOR MY FAMILY.
BECAUSE THEY WANTED TO PROTECT ME, THEY'D STOPPED ALL COMMUNICATION. THEY NEVER WANTED ME TO BE FOUND OUT.
BUT AFTER LEARNING THE TRUTH, I DIDN'T CARE ABOUT HIDING ANYMORE.
HUH? WHAT'S THAT?
AND THAT'S WHEN I FOUND . . .
HELLO?

HER. . . .

WHAT BRINGS YOU HERE?

I'M LEON, A FAIRY DEMON, AND I DISGUISE MYSELF IN PLUMERIA CITY AS A MEMBER OF THE FAIRY GUARD. I WAS HOPING TO FIND MY FAMILY, WHO WAS EXILED.

PLEASE, DO YOU KNOW ANYTHING ABOUT WHERE THEY COULD BE?

WHILE MY FAMILY WAS STILL NOWHERE TO BE FOUND . . .
EVA SHARED WITH ME HER GRAND PLAN TO SOMEDAY RE-CREATE THE WORLD AS ONE WHERE FAIRY DEMONS WOULD BE ACCEPTED—AND ALSO HAVE THEIR OWN CITY.

WITH A PLAN LIKE THAT, I FIGURED IT WOULD JUST BE A MATTER OF TIME UNTIL I REUNITED WITH MY FAMILY.
IN THE MEANTIME, I HAD TO CONTINUE PLAYING "FAIRY" TO GET BY IN PLUMERIA CITY.
I WORKED ALONGSIDE EVA, THINKING WE'D SOON BUILD A PERFECT WORLD FOR FAIRY DEMONS.
BUT AFTER SHE POISONED MOUNT MAGMA, I REALIZED THE TRUE STRENGTH OF HER UNIQUE POWERS. . . .

THEN SHE STARTED TEARING DOWN THE FORESTS OF PONDEROSA . . .
AND BUILT A LASER WITH THE PURPOSE OF DESTROYING PLUMERIA CITY AND THREATENED TO HURT ALL OF YOU. . . .
I THOUGHT OTHER FAIRY DEMONS WOULD STEP IN TO STOP HER . . .
BUT HER POWERS MAKE US TOO AFRAID TO SAY ANYTHING.

WELL, WE WANT TO HELP THE FAIRY DEMONS, TOO, BUT . . .

HOW CAN WE MAKE SURE THAT THIS ISN'T ANOTHER ONE OF YOUR LIES?

HUH?

HERE, I STOLE HER PLAN STRAIGHT FROM THE LAIR.
WHOA . . .
IT SHOWS HOW EVERYTHING IS CONNECTED—AND HOW TO STOP IT.

THAT POWER FROM HER HANDS . . .
IS THE SAME POISON THAT TOOK OVER MOUNT MAGMA.
I DON'T KNOW HOW SHE REFINED THE ABILITY, BUT SHE TRANSFUSED IT INTO THE LASER TO AMPLIFY ITS STRENGTH. IT'S NO LONGER POISONOUS TO THE TOUCH . . .
BUT HER HANDS ARE THE ONLY ONES THAT CAN CONTROL THE LASER.
BUT . . . WHY DO YOU NEED US?
WHY DON'T YOU JUST TAKE HER DOWN YOURSELF?

YOU KNOW EVA BEST AND YOU SAW WHAT SHE DID TO MY FANG.
YES, BUT I CAN'T MAKE HER CHANGE.
I DO BELIEVE, THOUGH, THAT THERE'S A LINK BETWEEN EVA'S EMOTIONS AND HER POWERS.
AND I BELIEVE YOU ARE THE ONES WHO CAN CHANGE THE WAY SHE FEELS.

AND I KNOW THAT'S SOMETHING YOU CAN DO, EVEN WITHOUT YOUR FANG. I SAW IT WHEN YOU SAVED MOUNT MAGMA.
PLUMERIA CITY AND MOUNT MAGMA ARE WORKING TOGETHER NOW, THANKS TO YOU.
I'LL NEED THE HELP OF EVERYONE, INCLUDING THE FAIRY DEMONS.
WELL . . .

YEAH, YOU'VE GOTTA GET THEM ON OUR SIDE, LEON!
THEY'RE BEING BRAINWASHED, TOO, AFTER ALL.
YES.
OK, THEN WHAT?
I JUST NEED EVA TO BE HELD OFF WHEN I SPEAK TO HER.
AND I THINK I KNOW SOMEONE WHO CAN HELP WITH THAT. . . .
OH, YEAH! OF COURSE!
I CAN HELP, TOO!

I GUESS I WAS WRONG ABOUT YOU TALKING TO FLOWERS. . . .
AND I'M GLAD YOU CAN PUT YOUR DEMON SKILLS TO USE AGAIN.
OK, I CAN TRY TO HOLD EVA OFF WITH MY CRYSTAL POWERS. SHE'LL WANT TO ACTIVATE THE LASER QUICKLY WHEN SHE FIGURES OUT WHAT WE'RE TRYING TO DO.
CHAI, YOUR FAMILY CAN STALL THE CONSTRUCTION WORKERS.
THE OBJECTIVE IS TO KEEP HER IN PLACE SO MEESH CAN FIND A WAY TO APPEAL TO HER EMOTIONS.
ALL RIGHT, LET'S GO AHEAD AND REHEARSE.

HERE'S THE FINAL PIECE TO COMPLETE THE LASER. PLEASE BE CAREFUL AS YOU CARRY THIS OUT.

IF YOU'RE NOT CAREFUL,
IT COULD POISON YOU, TOO.
AND YOU'RE STILL SURE
ABOUT THIS WHOLE PLAN?
DO YOU
DOUBT ME?
UH . . . NO.
I'M ON MY WAY TO
ATTACH THIS IMMEDIATELY.

WITH LEON ON THEIR SIDE NOW, THERE'S NO TELLING HOW MUCH TIME WE HAVE LEFT.
YES, I'LL GET THIS DONE AS SOON AS POSSIBLE.

IT SEEMS LIKE THEY'RE ALMOST DONE WITH THE LASER. . . .
REMEMBER THE PLAN, OK?
ON THE COUNT OF THREE . . .
HUH?

RUSTLE
REMEMBER OUR PLAN B!
I KNEW SHE'D GET TO US FIRST!
LEON!

I KNEW IT, YOU TRAITOR!
MOM?!
GRANDMA?!
WAIT, MOM! STOP! WE'RE OK! HE'S ON OUR SIDE!
WHAT . . . ?

LEON WAS DRAGGED INTO THIS BY THE FAIRY-DEMON LEADER.
AND HE SAVED ALL OF US FROM HER! HE SHOWED US THE PLAN SO WE'D KNOW HOW TO STOP IT.
REGARDLESS, I AM SORRY FOR LETTING YOU DOWN, YOUR HIGHNESS. PLEASE KNOW I PLAN TO HELP STOP ALL OF THIS BEFORE IT REACHES PLUMERIA CITY.
IT'S ALL RIGHT. IT WAS MY RESPONSIBILITY TO PREVENT THIS.
BUT I'M GLAD NOUNA ALREADY KNOWS WHAT TO DO.

OH, YOU DON'T NEED THAT SILLY OLD THING ANYWAY.

I . . . DON'T?
FANG OR NO FANG, WE'RE ALL TAKING THIS ON TOGETHER.
WE'VE ALREADY COME UP WITH A PLAN, TOO.
WHAT PLAN?
. . .
WOOO!

ONE . . . TWO . . .
THREE . . .
WHOOSH

AWOOO!!!

WOLVES?!

AH!

WHAT THE!

LET GO OF ME!

THANKS, CHAI!

OOF!
HUH?
THERE'S BEEN A CHANGE OF PLANS.

I'M PRETTY SURE
THIS IS THE ENTRAN–

WHOA!

THE ACID-PUKING
CLASS REALLY CAME
IN HANDY!

IT SURE IS DARK IN HERE. . . .
WELL, AT LEAST MY EYES CAN STILL SEE IN THE DARK.
MAYBE I'M NOT THAT USELESS AFTER ALL.
I TOLD YOU, MEESH, YOU STILL GOT IT!
I THINK IT'S DOWN THIS WAY. . . .

YEP, THERE IT IS . . .
ONCE IT EMERGES, THE LASER WILL START.
THE UNDERGROUND CITY.
YOU HEAR THAT?

WATCH OUT!!
XAVIER!
AH!
IT'S BEEN A WHILE, XAVIER. . . .

Y-YOU!!!

HA!!!

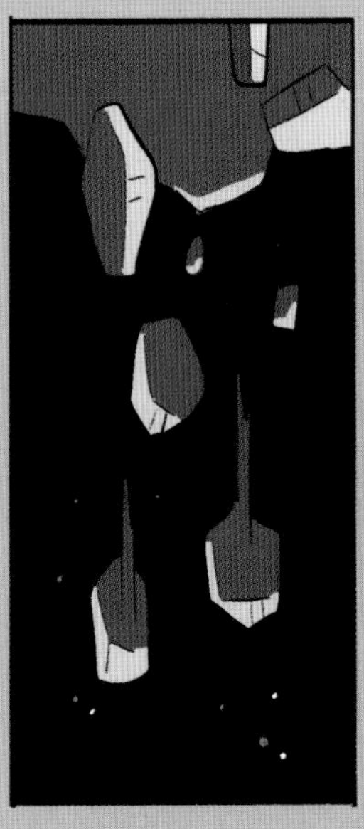

YOU WON'T GET AWAY WITH THIS!

AH!

XAVIER, WATCH OUT, SHE'LL . . .

GAH!

HEH, I SEE YOU'VE IMPROVED SINCE THE LAST TIME WE MET.
YOU OK?
BUT YOU'VE STILL GOT A LONG WAY TO GO.
AND I CAN ALSO PLAY THIS GAME FAIRLY.
DEMON TO DEMON.
MEESH, LOOK OUT!
HA!

I REALLY DID IT! A SHIELD!
MEESH!! WHERE ARE YOU GOING?
OOF!

AH!
NOUNA! NOW!
NOT SO FAST!

YOU THINK . . .
HEY!
WHERE'S SHE GOING?
THIS WILL STOP ME?
EVA!!! WE JUST WANT TO TALK!
OK, KIDS, WE HAVE TO RUN FOR IT.
NOW!
BUT SHE'S GONNA . . .

CRSH

THAT MEANS THE LASER, IT'S . . .
WE'LL WORRY ABOUT THAT ONCE WE GET OUT OF HERE!
DUCK!
AHHHHHH!
UGH . . .
MEESH!
THE LASER!

IT STARTED . . .

THERE IT IS!

THE LASER, IT'S COMING!

IT'S SO RAPID.
IT'S TEARING PLUMERIA CITY'S CLOUDS APART!

OK, ASSEMBLE IN PLACE!

PUT UP YOUR SHIELDS!
LET'S FORM A BIG ONE TOGETHER!
WILL THAT REALLY BLOCK IT?
WE'LL DIE TRYING IF WE HAVE TO!

AND WHAT HAPPENS
IF THIS DOESN'T WORK?
I...
FWSHHH
DON'T
KNOW.

LET THE CITY RISE!
BE CAREFUL WITH THE DEBRIS!
CHAI!
WATCH OUT FOR THE MACHINE!
CHAI!
ARE YOU OK?

AHH!
NO! XAVIER!
IT'S TOO BAD. . . .
XAVIER!!!

YOU ALL HAD YOUR CHANCE TO RUN. . . .
AH!
NOUNA!
GAH!

COME ON, NOUNA, WE HAVE TO GET YOU OUT OF HERE!

MEESH, AS YOUR GRANDMOTHER, I'M ORDERING YOU TO LISTEN!

WE CAN'T JUST LEAVE NOW! THE LASER WILL–

THE CITY . . . HAS ALREADY EMERGED, WHICH MEANS THE LASER IS ON ITS WAY TO DESTROY PLUMERIA CITY.
I KNEW THIS WAS A BAD IDEA!
AND THAT'S WHY WE STILL HAVE TO MAKE THINGS RIGHT!
BUT . . .
WHAT IF SHE KILLS US FIRST?
IT WON'T HAPPEN. NOT UNDER THE GUARDIAN'S WATCH.
YOU MEAN THAT KID?

COME ON, WE GOTTA MOVE! HER POWER IS BUILDING UP IN THAT CRYSTAL BALL FAST!

OH NO . . .
WHOA!
MEESH!

OOF!
RRRRR

A VORTEX?!
MEESH, RUN!
KAPOOM

HUH?!
MOM! NO!

KEEP STRENGTHENING THAT SHIELD!
WE CAN DO THIS!
HUH?
THE PALACE'S WING LIGHTS . . .
THEY'RE FLICKERING.

THE QUEEN . . .
COME ON, GUARDS, STAND YOUR GROUND!
THIS LASER'S GONNA HAVE TO GO THROUGH US FIRST!
FOR PLUMERIA CITY!
KSHHH

WHAT . . . ?
MOM!
MOM, WAKE UP!
PLEASE! IT'S ME! NOUNA!
GRANDMA!

UGH . . .
XAVIER . . .
CHAI . . .
THE LASER, IT'S GOING! IT'S ALREADY TORN SO MUCH APART.
THIS IS ALL MY FAULT. . . .
AND THAT'S WHY YOU SHOULD'VE JUST STAYED OUT OF IT.

WHY DO YOU EVEN WANT TO SAVE THESE WORLDS . . . WHAT HAVE THEY EVER DONE FOR YOU?!
MOUNT MAGMA REJECTED YOU. PLUMERIA CITY REJECTED YOU.
I KNOW WHAT YOU WENT THROUGH IN THOSE CITIES.
MAYBE I THOUGHT . . .
I HAD THE POWER TO CHANGE THINGS FOR THE BETTER.

BUT EVEN WHEN I'M SUPPOSED TO BE THE GUARDIAN . . . I STILL END UP HURTING EVERYONE. . . .
HERE, TAKE ME. DO WHATEVER YOU WANT.
JUST PROMISE YOU WON'T HURT ANYONE ELSE.
I'M DONE TRYING TO BE SOMEONE I'M NOT ENOUGH TO BE.

WHY DON'T YOU SHOW THE CLASS HOW TO FIRE-BREATHE THEN?!
YOU'RE SKIPPING CLASS TO TALK TO A FLOWER?!

CRSH
DEMON!!!
WE DON'T JUST LET ANYONE IN!
A DEMON WHO PLAYS WITH FAIRY TOYS?!

MEESH . . .
XAVIER?
I'M SORRY FOR WHAT I'VE PUT YOU THROUGH.
THOSE VOICES IN YOUR HEAD? IT'S ALL FROM US. IT'S NOT TRUE.
AND YOU DON'T NEED TO BE THE GUARDIAN . . .
TO BE A GOOD DEMON.

GUARDIAN? NO THANKS. BEING A MOM KEEPS ME BUSY ENOUGH!
WELCOME TO MY CAFÉ!
I JUST WANTED TO SPEND TIME WITH YOU.
I STUDIED SO HARD, BUT I COULD NEVER GET LAVA MOLDING RIGHT.
THE PRINCESS NOUNA YOU SEE ON TV ISN'T REAL.

WHAT THE—!
OW! YOU'RE CRUSHING MY HAND!
THERE'S NO WAY YOU CAN BE THAT STRONG. . . .

I'M THE GUARDIAN.
THAT SIMPLY CAN'T BE. . . .

ZZZZZZ
WHAT'S GOING ON?
WHAT . . . MEESH!
I KNEW SHE HAD IT IN HER ALL ALONG!
THAT'S MY LITTLE DEMON.

AH!
LEON! NOW!

I'M ONLY KEEPING THE PROMISE YOU MADE US, EVA.
WHAT?!
LEON . . .
NOW COME ON, LET'S RAISE THIS CITY HIGHER.
WE GOT THIS!
HNG!
COME ON!
NO WAY . . .

BZZZ
HUH? WE'RE FREED?!
CRK
MEESH STOPPED HER!
CRK
WHERE DID THE LASER GO?!
HOLD YOUR SHIELDS—IT MIGHT COME BACK!
HUH?

WHAT IS THAT?!
ARE THOSE . . . FAIRY DEMONS?
ARE THEY LIFTING THE CITY? THE GREEN STRIPES ARE DISAPPEARING!
PRINCESS?!
WE GOT THIS, TEAM!

DON'T TELL ME YOUR CITY WAS GOING TO BE CLOUDLESS!
LET'S GET YOU TO SAFETY, MA'AM.
BE CAREFUL OF THE DEBRIS!

YOU MUST BE EXHAUSTED FROM FLYING . . .
AND LIFTING!
YOU . . .
REALLY DID THAT.

AFTER WHAT I'VE DONE . . . WHY?
YOU MAY HAVE HURT OTHERS.
BUT I BELIEVE THERE'S STILL GOOD IN YOU.
ALL YOU WANTED WAS A PLACE FOR FAIRY DEMONS TO CALL HOME.

AND EVEN THOUGH YOU TOOK AWAY OURS . . .
YOU CAN NEVER TAKE AWAY FAMILY.
I HOPE SOMEDAY . . .
YOU CAN FIND YOURS.

IS THAT . . .

PRINCESS NOUNA?!

WHAT HAPPENED?! ARE YOU ALL RIGHT?! WHERE'S THE QUEEN?

MOM'S OK. SHE'S GOT A FEW BRUISES, BUT I'LL EXPLAIN ALL THAT LATER.
FIRST THINGS FIRST.
WE HAVE TO MAKE THINGS RIGHT . . .
WITH THE FAIRY DEMONS.

ONE MONTH LATER . . .

FAIRY DEMONS WERE WELCOMED BACK TO PLUMERIA CITY, IF THEY CHOSE TO RETURN.
NOW CREATURES OF ALL SORTS COULD MAKE HOMES HERE.
IT WASN'T JUST A FAIRY REALM ANYMORE.

AND NOUNA STUDIOS . . .
BECAME A NEW PLACE TO SHOWCASE THE TALENTS OF CREATURES FROM EVERYWHERE.
THE QUEEN RECOVERED AND HAPPILY WATCHED HER DAUGHTER CHANGE PLUMERIA CITY.
YOU MUST BE SO PROUD OF HER.

AS FOR THOSE WHO DARED TO ENTER MOUNT MAGMA . . .
THEY WERE WELCOMED BACK, TOO.
AND THAT'S WHAT BRINGS ME HERE!
SO, MEESH, WHAT IS THE BIGGEST THING YOU'VE LEARNED AS GUARDIAN?
WELL, I'VE LEARNED THAT BEING THE GUARDIAN ISN'T EVERYTHING.

WELCOME TO MOUNT MAGMA!
SURE, IT'S HANDY TO HAVE FRIENDS WITH POWERS AND TO WORK TOGETHER, BUT NOTHING IS MORE POWERFUL THAN BEING MYSELF.
IT FEELS GOOD TO BE SURROUNDED BY THOSE WHO ACCEPT ME FOR ME—AND DON'T ONLY SEE ME AS A GUARDIAN.
THANKS FOR TAKING CARE OF THE LAWN, KIDS!
AND MOST IMPORTANTLY, I'VE LEARNED THE POWER OF KINDNESS.
YOU SHOULD SHOW IT, EVEN TO THOSE WHO HAVE HURT YOU.
WE'LL TAKE IT FROM HERE. THANK YOU, MEESH!

WE ALL MAY BE CAPABLE OF MISTAKES . . .

BUT THE WILL TO FIX THEM IS WHAT SHOWS OTHERS WHO WE ARE.

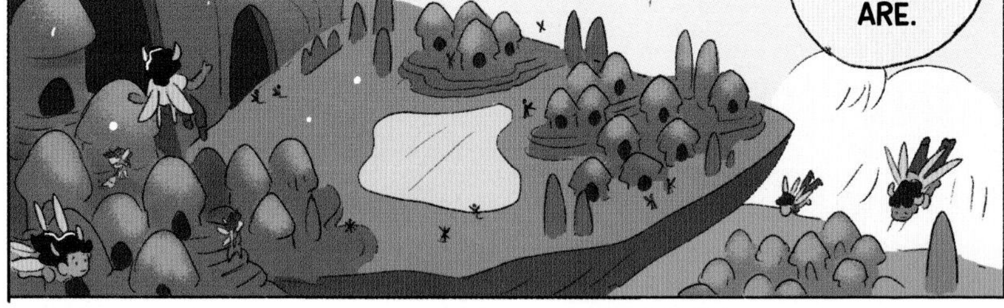

PONDEROSA

THANKS A LOT FOR THE NEW HOUSE! YOU DIDN'T HAVE TO, BUT . . .

HUH?

PLEASE, IT'S THE LEAST WE COULD DO AFTER ALL WE'VE DONE. AGAIN, WE'RE VERY SORRY.

UHH . . .

WHAT ARE YOU . . . ?

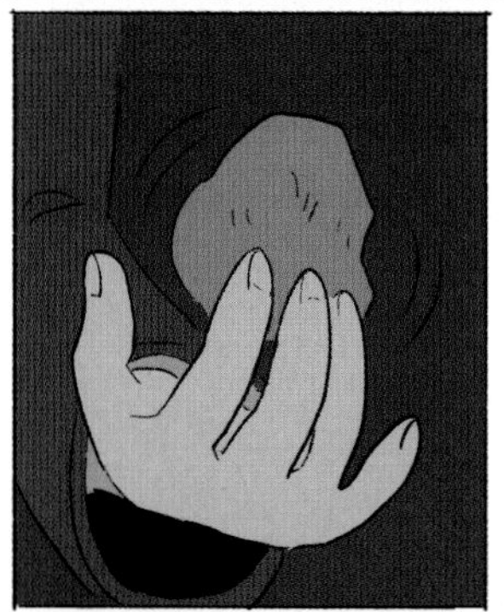

OH, A KEY?

WELL, I'M HAPPY TO HAVE SOME FAIRY-DEMON NEIGHBORS.

AND I'M SURE THEY'LL BE HAPPY TO HAVE YOU AS THEIRS, TOO.

OK, COME ON, EVA. IT'S TIME TO GO.
GO WHERE?
I'M OFF TO FIND MY FAMILY, AND EVA IS GOING TO RETURN TO HER AUNT AND UNCLE. BUT DON'T WORRY, THE OTHER FAIRY DEMONS WILL TEND TO THE REST OF THE CITY'S COMPLETION.
I HEARD THEY'LL EVEN BE BUILDING BRIDGES BETWEEN REALMS.
HOPEFULLY WHEN WE COME BACK WITH OUR FAMILIES, THEY'LL BE DONE.
BUT FOR NOW, TAKE CARE.

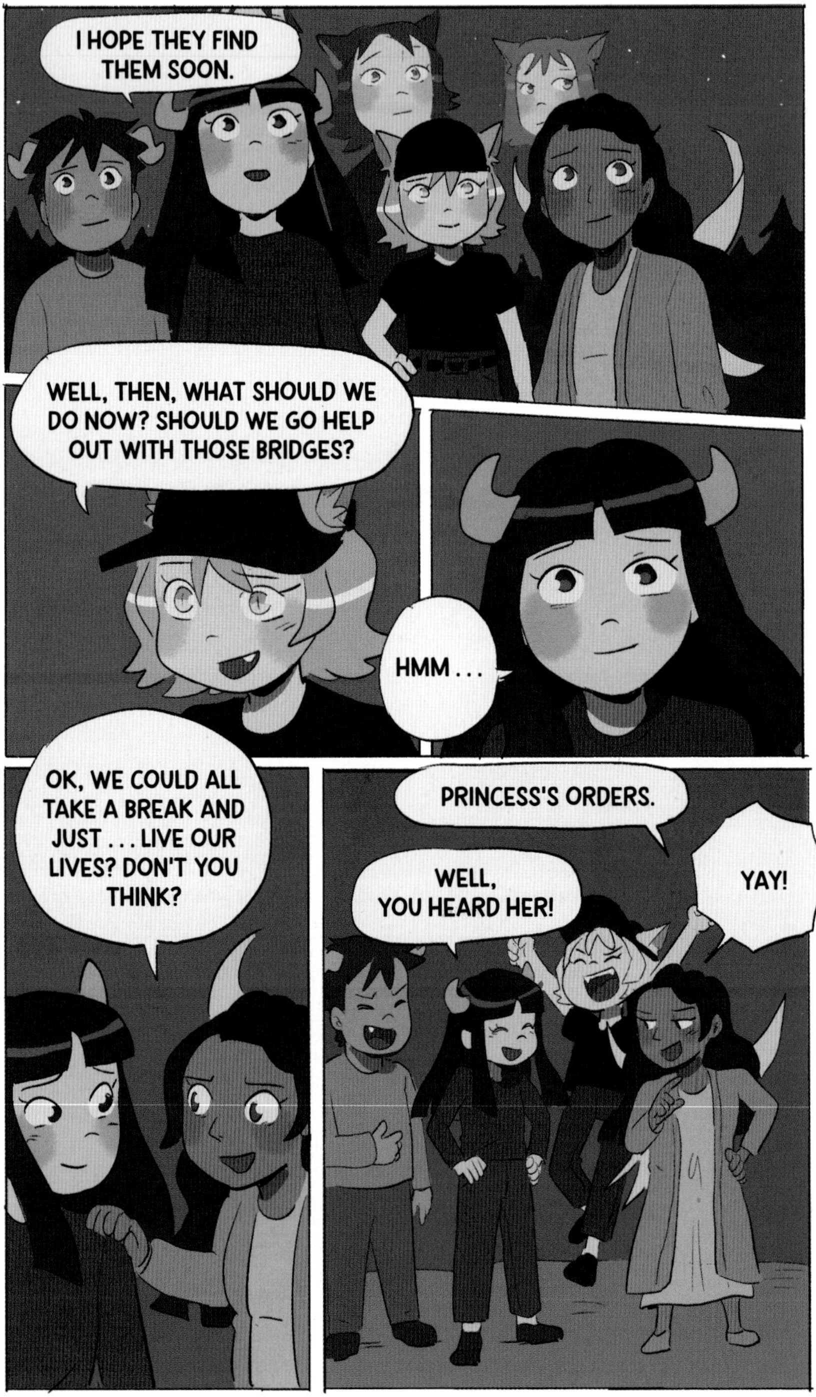

I HOPE THEY FIND THEM SOON.

WELL, THEN, WHAT SHOULD WE DO NOW? SHOULD WE GO HELP OUT WITH THOSE BRIDGES?

HMM . . .

MOST DEMONS MAY NOT BELIEVE THEIR GUARDIAN LOVES TO PLAY GAMES . . .
OR THAT SHE LOVES TO WATER FLOWERS . . .
OR IS FRIENDS WITH THE FAIRY PRINCESS, WEREWOLVES, AND HER FORMER SCHOOL BULLY.
BUT WHAT DOES THAT MATTER . . .

IF THE ONLY ONE WHO NEEDS TO BELIEVE IN HER . . .

IS ME?

THE MAKING OF Meesh the BAD DEMON

FIRST, I HAD TO BRAINSTORM A BUNCH OF DIRECTIONS WHERE THIS STORY COULD GO.

NO MATTER WHAT, IT WAS ALWAYS GOING TO BE ABOUT A DEMON GIRL TRYING TO DO GOOD.

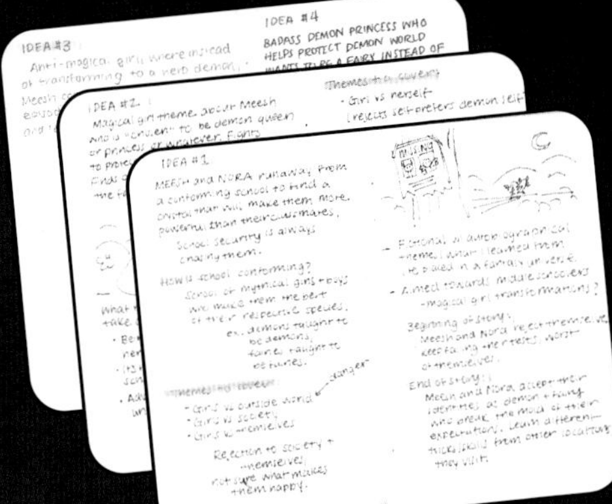

I THEN SKETCHED UP SOME CONCEPTS OF MEESH. AT THE TIME SHE WAS OLDER, BUT WE MADE HER YOUNGER TO RESONATE MORE WITH MIDDLE-GRADE STUDENTS.

IT WAS FUN TO THINK ABOUT ALL THE POSSIBLE CHARACTERS WHO COULD FIT IN THE MEESH WORLD, BUT UNFORTUNATELY, MANY OF THEM DID NOT MAKE IT! (WHICH IS GOOD BECAUSE IT SAVED MY HAND FROM DYING. HAHA.)

SINCE MOUNT MAGMA AND PLUMERIA CITY ARE TWO OF THE MAIN CITIES FEATURED IN THE STORY, I TOOK A RENDERED PASS AT THEM TO UNDERSTAND THE VIBE OF EACH CITY.

Meesh the Bad Demon Vol. 2
Story Outline

Synopsis:
Meesh learns to balance the power within herself vs. the Guardian fang while on a mission to find the one behind the poisoning of Mt. Magma

Act I

- Meesh adjusts back to life in Mt. Magma with the new identity of the Guardian attached to her. Grandma tries to train Meesh in ways to improve her skills as the Guardian, but also dives deeper into why she quit being the Guardian. She opens up about Meesh's mother.
    - Meesh barely has any memory of her mother, other than knowing she died early.
    - Grandma stopped being the Guardian because she felt her lack of attention while being the Guardian contributed to Meesh's mother's death, promising to never be like that again with Meesh.
    - "While being the Guardian brings you a lot of power and respect, never forget those who matter to you the most," Grandma says.
- Meesh continues to hang out with Nouna, Chai, and Xavier. The urgency to help Chai's family grows as they have run out of resources from their original home.
- Meesh and their friends either persuade their parental figures to go out and help Chai, or escape on their own to go on this mission.

Act II

- The male fairy guard has been observing Nouna and her friends all along, while reporting back to Eva, the demon-fairy.
    - The fairy guard has been secretly working alongside Eva, who has been constructing a giant machine on the grounds where Chai's family once lived.
    - Eva's goal is to lessen/eliminate creature prejudice by creating a machine that will emit a worldwide curse that will turn all "pure" creatures into "mixed" creatures.
- Meesh and her friends confront Eva's workers for the first time after discovering the construction grounds that took over Chai's family home. They discover that all the workers are mixed creatures, with the majority being demon-fairies.
- Eva surprises the gang, kidnapping Meesh, and leaving the rest of the gang behind. Nouna takes the lead to find Meesh from this point onward.

AFTER GATHERING ENOUGH IDEAS, IT WAS TIME TO STRUCTURE THEM INTO AN OUTLINE. WE WOULD REVISE THIS A FEW TIMES TO GET THE STORYLINE IN PLACE.

ONCE THE OUTLINE WAS APPROVED, I MOVED ON TO ROUGH SKETCHES.

THIS STAGE ALLOWS ME TO GET A FEEL FOR THE PACING AND THE DIALOGUE.

AFTER THE ROUGH SKETCHES ARE MIRACULOUSLY APPROVED, I MOVE ON TO FINAL LINE ART.

NOW THERE'S A CLEAR PICTURE OF WHAT'S GOING ON IN EACH SCENE!

THE LINE ART THEN GETS PASSED TO THE AMAZING COLORIST, WHO TIES EVERYTHING TOGETHER WITH EFFECTS AND LIGHTING!

LASTLY, MEESH GETS PRINTED AND BOUND INTO A REAL BOOK.

THANK YOU FOR READING MEESH THE BAD DEMON!